THIS WALKER BOOK BELONGS TO:

First published 1986 by Walker Books Ltd
87 Vauxhall Walk, London SE11 5HJ

This edition published 1991

© 1986 Nick Butterworth

Printed in Hong Kong by
Sheck Wah Tong Printing Press Ltd

British Library Cataloguing in Publication Data
Jill the farmer and her friends.
I. Title
823'.914[J]
ISBN 0-7445-1760-5

JILL THE FARMER

AND HER FRIENDS

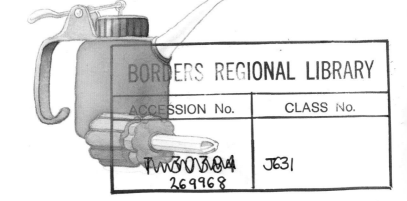

NICK BUTTERWORTH

WALKER BOOKS

LONDON

Jill is a farmer.

What does she drive?

Tom is a greengrocer.

What does he sell?

Anna is a doctor.

Why has she come?

Ben is an astronaut.

What does he control?

Diana has a shoe shop.

What does she sell?

Fred is a dustman.

What does he collect?

Nelly is a dressmaker.

What does she use?

Jim is a messenger.

What does he ride?

Betty is a baker.

What does she sell?

Pete is a mechanic.

What does he use?

MORE WALKER PAPERBACKS
For You to Enjoy

MY LITTLE BOOK OF COLOURS
MY LITTLE BOOK OF NUMBERS
by Jan Ormerod
Attractive first concept books by one of the most popular of
all children's picture book artists.
ISBN 0-7445-1473-8   *Numbers*
ISBN 0-7445-1474-6   *Colours*
£2.50 each

JOJO'S REVENGE
by Mick Inkpen
Baby Jojo is tired of being squeezed, prodded and passed
around like a parcel. Now he's going to have his revenge!
"A must… A baby's eye view of life with succinct wit and
clear, genuinely comic drawings." *The Observer*
ISBN 0-7445-1709-5   £2.99